Miss Wondergem's
Dreadfully Dreadful Pie

BY
VALERIE SHERRARD

ILLUSTRATED BY
WENDY J. WHITTINGHAM

Canada Council Conseil des Arts
for the Arts du Canada

Canada

Newfoundland
Labrador

We gratefully acknowledge the financial support of the Canada Council for the
Arts, the Government of Canada through the Canada Book Fund (CBF),
and the Government of Newfoundland and Labrador through the Department of Tourism,
Culture and Recreation for our publishing program.

Cover Design by Todd Manning
Layout by Joanne Snook-Hann
Printed on acid-free paper

Published by
TUCKAMORE BOOKS
an imprint of CREATIVE BOOK PUBLISHING
a Transcontinental Inc. associated company
P.O. Box 8660, Stn. A
St. John's, Newfoundland and Labrador A1B 3T7

Printed in Canada by:
TRANSCONTINENTAL INC.

Library and Archives Canada Cataloguing in Publication

Sherrard, Valerie
    Miss Wondergem's dreadfully dreadful pie / Valerie Sherrard ; Wendy Whittingham,
illustrator.

ISBN 978-1-897174-81-4

    I. Whittingham, Wendy II. Title.

PS8587.H3867M57 2011   jC813'.6   C2011-905319-5

*To my family for all their love and support,
and to V with utmost gratitude.*
– W.J.W.

Myrna and Verna and Bradley McGrew
Loved skating and movies and trips to the zoo.

Every day, every way, they were happy at play –
From the first day of June to the last day of May.

Their lives were a frolic of laughter and fun.
And as for their problems – they had only one!
For Mother McGrew, though she cared for them well,
Was a *terrible* cook – you could tell by the smell.

Her cookies and muffins and pies were so hard,
That they used them for building a fort in the yard.
I would venture to say, and believe it's the truth,
That a buttermilk biscuit cost Verna a tooth.

The very best food Mother made was a stew,
Which rather resembled a gooey grey glue.
The children protested, they griped, they implored,
For tastier meals but their pleas were ignored.

Then one sunny day in the middle of June,
Through the centre of town came a lazy balloon.
It floated along with its head in the air
And a message in gold written boldly in flair.

The bright balloon flew by the children McGrew.
They read it aloud as it came into view:
"Miss Wondergem's Bakery, coming quite soon!
In fact, it will open tomorrow at noon!"

The trio McGrew gave a squeal of delight!
An answer, at last, to their terrible plight.
And so the next day at a quarter to four
The children rushed into Miss Wondergem's store.

They ordered pink cupcakes with sprinkles on top,
(If there were no sprinkles, they'd take a gumdrop)
Some cookies with oatmeal and raisins and dates,
And brownies – enough to fill up several plates.

When all of their orders were eagerly placed,
(Which didn't take long, for they spoke with great haste)
Miss Wondergem sighed and she shook her small head,
She wrung her wee hands and her tiny voice said:

"I'm sorry. I have neither sprinkles nor dates,
No cookies or brownies to heap upon plates.
I only make pies. Pies are all I can make.
I missed a few classes when I learned to bake."

A bakery with nothing but pies? How bizarre!
Then Myrna spoke up, she said, "We've come this far!
So – I'll have a light, fluffy lemon chiffon."
And Bradley decided that he'd have pecan.

Then Verna said, "Apple – no wait! Make it peach!"
But what they heard next was a sad blow to each...
"I never use peaches or lemons or nuts,
And my chiffons fall, I'm a bit of a klutz."

She might have said more but the bakery door,
Flew open and in came a fellow who bore

Two bundles, three parcels a box and a bag –
Each one with a "Speedy Delivery" tag.

"Good day!" said the chap, "I have brought your supplies,
All the things that you need to put into your pies.

One jar full of bat spit, the slime of six slugs,
The noses and ears from a wide range of bugs."

"Green lizard tongues, chopped up with scorpion tails,
The eyebrows from beetles and freshwater snails,

The finest of frog toes, the choicest of worms,
And lastly, there's something that gurgles and squirms."

I think you can guess – do I need to say more?
The children raced home – and they bolted their door!
They tried very hard, but they could not forget
What they heard on that day – it was awful, and yet...

A strange thing has happened, it's hard to explain –
At mealtime the children no longer complain.
They've grown rather fond of their mother's cuisine;
They smile as they eat and they leave their plates clean.

And as for the pies that Miss Wondergem made,
Demand for them grew through a mail-order trade.
She sends them to goblins, to trolls and to sprites,
Who call them Miss Wondergem's Tasty Delights!

ABOUT THE AUTHOR
Valerie Sherrard is an acclaimed children's and young adult author whose work has been shortlisted for numerous Canadian awards. Her insights into children come from years of working with them in various capacities, as well as fostering over seventy teens. Valerie lives in Miramichi, New Brunswick with her husband Brent and their four very spoiled cats.

ABOUT THE ILLUSTRATOR
Wendy J. Whittingham began drawing at the young age of two and was seldom seen without a pencil in hand. As she matured, her love of art inspired her to study further and she later graduated from the Graphic Design Program at Humber College as well as the Illustration Certificate Program at Sheridan College. Currently, Wendy shares a home with her husband George, three dogs, and two cats.